This book is a work of fiction. Any references to historical events, real people, or real places are used fictitiously. Other names, characters, places, and events are products of the author's imagination, and any resemblance to actual events or places or persons, living or dead, is entirely coincidental.

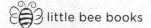 little bee books

An imprint of Bonnier Publishing USA
251 Park Avenue South, New York, NY 10010
Copyright © 2018 by Bonnier Publishing USA
All rights reserved, including the right of reproduction in whole or in part in any form. Little Bee Books is a trademark of Bonnier Publishing USA, and associated colophon is a trademark of Bonnier Publishing USA.

Library of Congress Cataloging-in-Publication Data
Names: Kent, Jaden, author. | Bodnaruk, Iryna, illustrator.
Title: The Dragon Games! / Jaden Kent; Iryna Bodnaruk.
Description: First edition. | New York, New York: Little Bee Books, [2019]
Series: Ella and Owen; [10] | Summary: Ella is magically sabotaged when she enters the Winged Wonders Flying Championship, and while she tries to undo the spell, Owen tries to clear his gremlin's name and find the real culprit.
Identifiers: LCCN 2018022833| Subjects: | CYAC: Contests—Fiction. | Sabotage—Fiction. | Dragons—Fiction. | Brothers and sisters—Fiction. | Twins—Fiction. | Magic—Fiction. | Humorous stories. | Classification: LCC PZ7.1.K509 Dp 2018 | DDC [Fic]—dc23 LC record available at https://lccn.loc.gov/2018022833

Printed in China TPL 0918
ISBN 978-1-4998-0617-5 (hc)
First Edition 10 9 8 7 6 5 4 3 2 1
ISBN 978-1-4998-0616-8 (pb)
First Edition 10 9 8 7 6 5 4 3 2 1

littlebeebooks.com
bonnierpublishingusa.com

ELLA AND OWEN

THE DRAGON GAMES!

by
Jaden Kent

little bee books

illustrated by
Iryna Bodnaruk

TABLE OF CONTENTS

1
TIME TO FLY

"I hope there will be elves at this thing," Owen said as he and his twin sister Ella flew through the forest. "I just *love* elves."

"I know! Stop talking about elves," Ella said. "I don't want to be late for the Dragon Games."

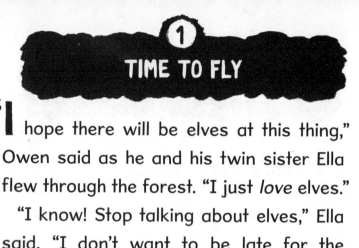

"We have time!" Owen said. "*Plenty* of time! Maybe I can buy a pointy elf hat . . . or pointy elf slippers!"

The two dragons flew through the woods near their home in Dragon Patch.

GONG!

"There's the first gong! The Winged Wonders Flying Championship is the first competition, and we're going to be late unless you flap faster!" Ella said.

"I'm flapping so fast, my scales are clattering together," Owen said. "And I'm all worn out. *And* I'm hungry!"

"We wouldn't have to hurry at all if your pet gremlin hadn't stolen your dumb book—"

"*The Adventures of Azerath the Blue Dragon* is a masterpiece!" Owen interrupted.

Ella continued, "And then traded it to some goblins for a stinky fish!" Ella took a deep breath.

Squeaky ran underneath the twin dragons, scampering over rocks and jumping over fallen trees in the forest. He struggled to keep up. "Huffa huffa puffa," Squeaky huffed.

"Hey, Squeaky's a good pet," Owen said. "Sort of."

"Well, his troublemaking nonsense is gonna make me late!" Ella said. "If I miss the first round, I'll be disqualified!"

"Don't worry!" Owen said. "You're still going to be there in time to compete . . . and see your hero, Clara Dragon Coleslaw."

"Xara Claw Wing!" Ella corrected. "She flew the Pixie Dust 500 race in record time last year. She's one of the best Wingers ever!"

"Do you really think you'll get to meet her?" Owen said.

"I'm not only going to meet her," Ella stated boldly, "I'm going to compete against her, and *beat* her!"

"Well, I'm going to meet some fried pumpkin burgers and beat them!" Owen licked his lips with his forked tongue.

BA-KONG! BONG! BONG!

That was the sound announcing that the Dragon Games were about to start!

Ella and Owen flew from the woods and headed toward the arena. Squeaky still scampered underneath them.

"We made it!" Ella cried out. "They haven't started yet!"

The gong *BONG*-ed again. It was even louder this time. Startled, Squeaky jumped into the air and bumped his head on Owen's belly.

"Ow!" Owen yelped. He tipped sideways and crashed into Ella. Startled, her wings stopped fluttering and she fell straight to the ground.

KA-PLOP!

Ella slid across the dirt and bonked her head on a rock, flipped over it, and tumbled claws over snout through the air.

"Yaaaaaaaah!" she screamed.

WHAM!

She landed on her back in front of the stone archway of the Dragon Games arena. Two young dragon competitors giggled as Ella lay on the ground.

"Very nicely done, wonder wings," Fangnir said. The bright blue dragon puffed a blast of steam from his slender nostrils. "Isn't that right, Avalon?"

Avalon giggled. "Save that energy for the games, honey," she said to Ella. Avalon was a bright orange dragon about the same size as Ella.

"I hope you're here for the 100-meter Fireball Toss," Fangnir said. "Cause we'll totally win that."

"Or maybe you'll enter the High-Flying Fire Hurdles of Flying Fire Competition," Avalon said. "Cause we'll win that, too."

Ella groaned as she stood up. She shook the dirt from her scales and fluttered her wings. "I'm Ella," she said. "And I'm here for the Winged Wonders Flying Championship."

"What-EVER!" the dragon duo said in unison. They started to walk away, but stopped as a red straw mat unrolled through the archway from behind them.

Grimly the Gnome marched down the mat with a large horn. When he reached the end, he stood in front of Ella and blew into his musical instrument as loudly as possible. His cheeks puffed out like his mouth was full of firebees and his scraggly red beard shook like a banner.

HORN! TRUMPET! FANFARE!

"Make way for the Winged Wonder herself, Xara Claw Wing!" A troll stepped aside as Xara Claw Wing walked through the crowd of dragons and stopped at the red mat where Ella stood.

"Ahem!" Xara Claw Wing cleared her throat. "I believe you are on the red mat . . . the *champion's* mat," she said to Ella.

Ella took a step back.

"Clara Xaw Wing?! I mean Wara Blaw Zing?! I mean Xara Claw Wing!" Ella blurted out like a nervous fairy. "Could I get a claw-tograph?"

"Sorry, kid," the champion said. "I simply don't do the claw-tograph thing anymore." Xara Claw Wing turned and strolled down the red mat and through the stone archway.

Ella heard the cheers from inside the arena as the crowd greeted the champion.

"She seems nice," Owen said. "Y'know, like any mean dragon does."

"She's a very busy and famous dragon," Ella explained to her brother. "So many things on her mind. Big things. Important things. And stuff."

"Yeah, like how to be a stuck-up dragon celebrity," Owen replied. "Look, Ella, this stuff is boring, and I'm super-bored by boring things being boring. I'm going to the marketplace to find something to eat. I'll be back to watch you fly."

"Eesa eesa eaty eat," Squeaky said.

"C'mon, Squeaky! I'm dying for a deep-fried beetle roll with antenna sauce." Owen and Squeaky headed to the marketplace, which was a row of wooden stalls with food, crafts, and some things even Owen couldn't identify.

And one of those things he couldn't identify was the shadowy figure who raced past Owen and accidentally stepped on his foot.

"Owww!" Owen cried out. He stopped and looked around, expecting an apology, but the claw-stepper had disappeared into the crowd.

"Get your maze on, dragon," a Minotaur called out to Owen. "No home is complete without its own maze!"

"Can you eat it?" Owen asked. "Is it a chocolate maze with nuts?"

The Minotaur snorted. "Don't be silly, dragon boy."

HATS FOR ALL

WOLF BERRY SM.. THIE

SWEET BUT STINKY FRUIT

Next to the Minotaur was a witch. She had a large wart on her forehead. "Care for some of my specialty?" she said. "A wart bigger-maker? It'll make all your warts bigger and better."

"That's nice, but I don't have any warts," Owen said.

"Well, I have a bottle of wart-maker, too," the witch said. She held up a bottle with a skull and crossbones on it. Green smoke puffed out from beneath its lid.

Squeaky reached for the bottle, but Owen pulled his hand away.

"I know what you need, my scaly friend," a dwarf called out from the next stall. "I've got homemade soap from the sap of the stickle-oak tree. It's guaranteed to pull the hair off your back. And your front, too!" she said.

"I have scales," Owen said, "so I don't need any hair removed."

Squeaky's tummy gurgled. "That's right, Squeaky," Owen said. "We need to find some food."

"Need food, got food, good food!" a voice called out.

Owen and Squeaky were suddenly face-to-face with a troll in a top hat, big rubber boots, and a poncho.

"Basher McBash," the troll said. "Me got food for you. Free food. Want to see food me have?"

"Do we ever!" Owen exclaimed.

Basher produced a large buttermelon from beneath his poncho. He placed it gently on the ground. Reaching into his poncho again, he pulled out a giant wooden mallet.

"Butter of melon . . . explode!" Basher yelled as he proceeded to bash the buttermelon with the mallet.

Juice and bits of buttermelon sprayed in all directions, covering Owen and Squeaky. Basher laughed.

"Now that's a free lunch!" Owen exclaimed.

Squeaky clapped his hands together. "Issa meena blaata boo!" he said.

WHO'S LAUGHING NOW?

The first round of the flying competition was already underway. Dragon after dragon took to the sky and did their best to fly through an obstacle course. Ella was the last to go. She was just finishing a loop-de-loop through the 3 Stone Hoops of Wonder when Owen returned to the arena, licking buttermelon juice from his claws.

Owen looked around and realized that Squeaky was nowhere to be seen. "Squeaky? Squeaky?" Owen called out. "I hope that crazy gremlin isn't getting me into more trouble."

The crowd cheered. Owen looked up and saw Ella soaring through the sky, her wings flapping like crazy as she spun through the last Stone Hoop.

"GOOOOOO, SIS!" Owen shouted and stamped his tail on the ground.

"Go, Ella! Go, Ella! Gooooo!" the crowd of dragons yelled. The dragons were totally on her side now.

Ella swirled around in the air. Her eyes caught something rustling in the bushes below, but by the time she swirled again, it was gone.

She swirled a third time, and this time, her eyes looked up toward the sun.

That always makes her sneeze, Owen thought, watching from the ground. And it did.

Ella sneezed. A blaze of fire shot out from her nostrils. She moved her snout around and scorched a heart shape into the ground.

The crowd cheered even louder.

Xara Claw Wing paced the field, scraping her claws into the ground with each step. "I hate it when other dragons try to steal my spotlight."

"Attention, all participants! The judges have made their decisions, and are ready to announce the final four contestants!" a dwarf judge called out.

Ella crossed her claws and closed her eyes. "Just say Ella . . . just say Ella . . . just say Ella," she whispered to herself.

Owen crossed his claws and closed his eyes, too. "Just say Ella . . . just say Ella . . . and let her win a deep-fried beetle roll with antenna sauce."

"The finalists are Xara Claw Wing, Avalon, Fangnir . . . and in her first Dragon Games, Stella!" the dwarf announced.

Ella gasped. The crowd looked around to see who was named Stella.

"Whoops, sorry," the dwarf said. "I mean, Ella! Ella is going to the Final Four."

Ella was thrilled. "Yes! I made the Final Four! I'm competing for the championship!"

"Congratulations," Xara said coldly, and turned and walked away.

Owen ran up to his sister. "She still seems . . . not nice."

"Oh, be quiet." Ella sniffed. "And why do you smell like buttermelon?"

"**Y**ou did it! You made the Final Four!" Owen congratulated his sister. "We can go home now, right?"

"Oh, please!" Ella replied. "I have to warm up for the championship."

"So we're not going home?"

"Dragon up!" Ella said. She took off into the air for her warm-up. She rolled to the left, rolled to the right, did two loop-de-loops, and was just about to try a barrel roll when—

A bolt of magical energy crackled around her. Her wings flapped faster, her scales tingled, and her claws curled. "I— I— what was *that*?" she said.

Ella zigged and zagged and flew out of the arena. She crashed to the ground. **KA-PLOPP!**

Owen raced out of the arena and bumped into a princess with long, golden hair, purple skin, and a matching purple dress. She wore a jeweled tiara on the top of her head.

"Excuse me, strange purple human princess," Owen said. "Have you seen my sister around here anywhere? She's an annoying dragon." Owen fluttered his wings. "With wings like these, only slower."

"Owen! Stop fooling around," the princess said. "It's me!"

"Ha-ha-ha. That's a good one," Owen replied. "No, my sister is a dragon, and look at you. You're a purple little human princess. I didn't even know humans came in purple."

The princess looked down at her hands. Her claws and scales were gone and in their place were slender human fingers. *Purple* fingers . . . the same color as her scales! The princess touched her face. Her dragon snout was now a perky little human nose.

"Noooooo!" Ella screamed. "I've been cursed! Where are my scales? My tail? My wings?"

"If you're really Ella, you'll know the answer to this question," Owen said. "What color is Azerath the dragon?"

"Will you stop talking about that crazy book!" Ella squeaked.

"Okay, you're Ella, all right! Mom and Dad will be so proud," Owen said. "They've always wanted to have royalty in the family."

"I don't want to be a *princess!*" she cried. "I want to be a dragon!" She grabbed her brother with her tiny human hands. "Who did this to me?! Who?!"

Squeaky ran up with a magic wand in his hand. "Zapp zappa zap zap!" Squeaky shook his body like he was struck by lightning and collapsed to the ground.

"Squeaky! I should've guessed!" Ella yelled. "Owen!"

"No," Owen said, defending Squeaky. "He's saying that he saw you get zapped by someone hiding in the bushes. That's the magic wand that did it. Either that or he now wants to wear a fish on his head as a hat."

"No way! I'm not believing it for one second," Ella said. "Gremlins are always up to no good. Get him to turn me back into a dragon RIGHT NOW!"

Squeaky shrugged. He waved the magic wand around in rapid circles. A few sparks shot out of the top, but nothing else happened. "Poo poo poo poopah," the gremlin said.

"I believe him," Owen said. "Magic spells and evil curses aren't a gremlin thing. Gremlins like to break plates and throw food."

"Argh!" Ella cried. "I've got to hide! No one can see me like this! What if they kick me out of the Dragon Games?!"

"You could be the star of the Running Around Like a Crazy Princess Games," Owen said.

"Quiet!" she said. "You've got to find me a cure before the championship starts!"

"And also prove Squeaky's innocence, right?" Owen said.

"Whatever!" Ella sighed. "And take a bath. You both stink of buttermelon."

"**D**on't worry, Squeaky. We'll prove that you didn't turn Ella into a princess, but first we need to find a way to turn her *back* into a dragon." Owen stopped and looked at Squeaky. "You *didn't* turn Ella into a princess, right?"

"Baaaata baaata beeeee baaaaa!" Squeaky angrily grumbled.

43

"I didn't understand a word you just said, but I hope that means 'no!'" Owen replied worriedly.

The duo hurried down the path until they arrived at the merchant stalls in the Dragon Games arena.

"Excuse me!" Owen said to a troll in the closest booth. "Any chance you have a counter-spell? My sister's been turned into a human."

"Me got just the thing!" the troll said and pointed to a large, silver pot. "Gremlin climb inside magic, happy, fun ride and problem solved!"

"That's not a ride," Owen said. "That's a *cooking pot*!"

"Yaaaaa!" Squeaky squealed and hid behind Owen's wings.

"No, no, no! It magic ride! Gremlin climb in. Gremlin lasagna come out in about one hour and twenty minutes. Maybe sooner if me make cooking fire bigger. Oops. Me mean make ride *fun* bigger," the troll answered.

"I think we'll pass," Owen said.

Owen and Squeaky talked to the Minotaur selling home maze kits, the witch selling wart enlarger, and the dwarf selling back hair remover, but no one could help them.

Owen was about to give up when he approached the last stall.

"YOU!" the man behind the table said the moment he saw Owen. It was Ken the grumpy wizard. "Go away before I turn you into a banana!"

Ken waved his wand about. It fired a magic bolt that zapped Ken's foot and turned it into a banana.

"Oh, wizard hats!" Ken growled. "Please tell me there are no monkeys anywhere around here."

"Look, my sister was turned into a princess," Owen explained. "I'm looking for a way to turn her back into a dragon. Can you help me?"

"If it'll get you to go away and never come back, then yes!" Ken grumbled. "Usually that would be more than enough for me, but you made me turn my foot into a banana, so I'm grumpy now."

"You're *always* grumpy," Owen said under his breath.

"If you want my help, you need to give me something," Ken said.

"My troll smells in a jar collection?" Owen asked.

"No. I need . . . your gremlin," Ken said.

"Eeeeeeeeee!" Squeaky squealed.

"Why do you want Squeaky?" Owen asked, confused.

"He can keep creatures like you from coming into my shop!" Ken explained.

"He would like that way too much," Owen replied.

"Eesa meena!" Squeaky agreed.

"**S**is! Sis!" Owen whispered. "I've got a surprise! Come on out!"

Ella peaked out from behind a large rock. "Did you find a counter-spell?!" she asked hopefully.

"I found something even better," Owen said. "Buuuut . . . it's a lot grumpier."

"I'm not an 'it,'" Ken said. "I am the great wizard known by the ancient name of . . . Ken."

"You must really have snails for brains if this is the best solution you could come up with," Ella said with a groan. "And why is his foot a banana?"

Ken hid behind Owen. "Ahhh!!! Do you see any monkeys nearby?!"

"It's not like I had a lot of choices! It was either a wart grower or a grumpy wizard," Owen defended.

"Grumpy or not, I'm a very busy wizard and my banana—I mean my foot—is already turning brown!" Ken said. "Can we get on with this?"

"What do I need to do?" Ella asked.

"Nothing. Just stand back and be prepared for the awesome magical magic of . . . Ken!" Ken waved his wand and shouted, "DRAGON KA-ZOWIE!"

The glass sphere on the top of the wand flew off the handle.

"That's a good thing, right?" Owen asked.

"Um . . . probably not," Ken admitted.

A bolt of purple magical energy covered Ella in a flash of blinding light. Ella looked at her arms. Nothing had changed, but now dragon wings stuck out from her back.

"Aaaaaaa! Now I'm even worse!" Ella screamed. "There is no way I'm gonna let the other dragons see me like this!"

"At least you're not a banana," Owen said, trying to be cheerful.

"But I'm still a princess!" Ella yelled.

"Nah . . . More like a dragoness! Or a princessagon!" Owen said.

"Hold on, I'll fix it." Ken hopped toward the marketplace on one foot so he wouldn't squish his banana foot. "I just need to get a stronger wand. Meet me at my stall!"

"There's not enough time anymore! The competition is going to start any minute now!" Ella slumped down. "Let's just go home."

"Go home?!" Owen gasped. "Did Azerath the Blue Dragon go home when the goblins of Goregath used a magic Scorn Cob to turn him into a very smelly shoe?"

"Yeah, I don't know. I never read that dumb book of yours," Ella said.

"Well, he didn't!" Owen paced back and forth, thumping his tail on the ground. "This isn't a dragon beauty contest! It's a dragon *flying* contest! You can't give up just because you look like a mutant princess with purple dragon wings!"

"I'm hoping that sounds worse than it looks, huh?" Ella asked.

"No, it actually looks *much* worse than it sounds," Owen replied. "You look totally freaky. But who cares? You're not a banana. So go out there and show them what a dragoness or uh, a princessagon, can do!"

BEHOLD THE FLYING DRAGONESS OR UH, PRINCESSAGON!

Trumpets blared! It was time for the championship round!

Xara soared into the sky! She flew past the lava blasters, did two loops, and arced into the clouds.

"Next comes the magical rings!" an ogre sitting next to Grimly said. "If her wings touch them, she'll be fried like a moss beetle fritter!"

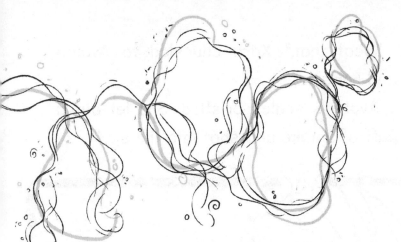

"Feh. Xara could do this with one wing tied behind her back!" Grimly chuckled.

Xara folded her wings against her back and dove through the magical rings that spun in the sky. Not a single dragon scale touched the glowing energy.

Xara dodged and twisted past obstacle after obstacle and finally landed amidst a puff of fire and smoke that she blew from her nostrils. The crowd erupted with shouts of joy, and no one cheered louder than Grimly the gnome.

"Beat that," Xara chuckled to Avalon and Fangnir.

Avalon's scales bristled. She let out a puff of smoke and shot into the sky!

Avalon zoomed through the flying course, but she singed her tail on the magic rings.

Fangnir went next. He scorched a wing on the lava obstacle, but he too made it through the course. He landed in front of Xara and dug his claws into the ground.

"Nice flying," Xara began, "but not good enough. I still have the fastest time."

"You're the best, Xara!" Grimly shouted from the crowd as he waved a XARA'S #1 sign over his bald head.

"I guess that other dragon, Smella, or whatever her name is, chickened out. Looks like I win . . . again." Xara smiled.

"Hold your scales!" Owen called out. "My sister, Smella—I mean Ella—is still gonna fly!"

"Holy tails! What happened to you?!" Xara laughed the moment she saw Ella. "I knew you were an ugly dragon before, but now you're an even uglier princess!"

"Uh, *hello*?" Owen said. "She's a dragoness."

"A dragoness?!" Grimly laughed from the crowd. "I'd rather be a *troll*!"

"WHAT?!" The trolls in the crowd turned and glared at Grimly.

"I mean, I uh, well, I'd rather be not-a-troll."

The trolls cheered. "Better," one said.

"Xara's kinda right," Avalon said.

"Yeah, you really are uglier now," Fangnir added.

"You shouldn't make fun of someone just because they look different," Ella said, getting angry.

"You're right," Grimly said. "So we'll laugh at you because you're so terrible at flying."

"I bet she flies like a fairy with her wings upside down!" Xara laughed.

Ella glared at Xara and adjusted the crown on her head.

"I have to admit, I like it when you look at someone like that," Owen said to Ella.

"Why?" Ella asked.

"Because it means you're about to kick some scales!" Owen said.

"You've got that right, bro!" Ella replied and zoomed into the sky.

Ella flapped her wings and flew toward the first obstacle: the lava blasters. Two trolls cranked handles on a machine that sprayed lava into the air. Ella banked left, toward the blasters. The trolls leapt into action! Lava shot into the sky! Ella flapped her wings as hard as she could, twisted her body this way and that, and zoomed between the lava streams.

"Can I look now?" Owen asked, holding
his claws over his eyes.

Ella would need to be even faster to get through the magical rings. She waited until the rings aligned, then shot through each one in a single breath.

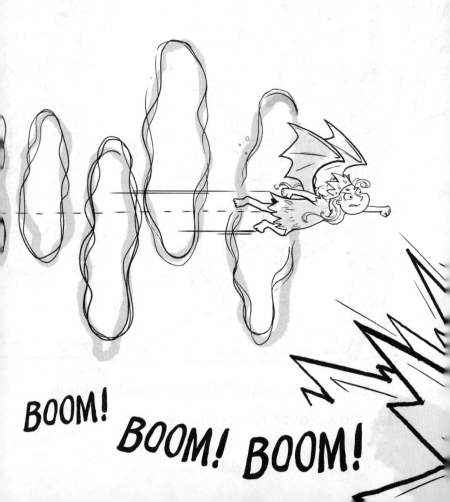

BOOM! BOOM! BOOM!

Lightning bolts exploded in the air all around Ella and nearly knocked her out of the sky. The next obstacle was a storm giant that was readying even bigger and scarier lightning bolts. Ella didn't have time to think. She folded her wings and dove toward the storm giant.

"Wha—what's she doing?!" Owen yelped.
"She's supposed to avoid the storm giant.
I can't look anymore!" Owen covered his
eyes again.

BOOM! BOOM! BOOM!

More lightning bolts exploded right next to Ella. She ducked down and flew between the storm giant's legs, surprising her. The storm giant lost her balance and crashed backward onto the mountain.

Like Xara, Fangnir, and Avalon had done before her, Ella dodged obstacle after obstacle until she came to the last one: the Cyclops!

Owen nervously bit his claws. "Oh, no! What's he gonna do? Shoot giant arrows at her?!"

"Worse," an ogre answered. "He's got a really, really big flyswatter."

Owen quickly covered his eyes again. "AAAAAAAAA! He's gonna splat my sister!"

The Cyclops was thirty feet tall and he was all that remained between Ella and the finish line. He pulled out an enormous flyswatter and swung it at Ella.

WHOOSH!

Ella dove to her left!

SPLAT!

The Cyclops missed Ella and accidentally swatted a group of elves having a picnic.

"Hey! Watch where you're swinging that thing!" an elf stuck to the flyswatter shouted angrily.

WHOOSH!

The Cyclops swung at Ella again. Ella bolted to the right, flying past the Cyclops and over the finish line.

The crowd went wild!

"Why is everyone cheering?!" a nervous Owen asked, too afraid to look. "Did Ella get swatted?! Am I an only child now?!"

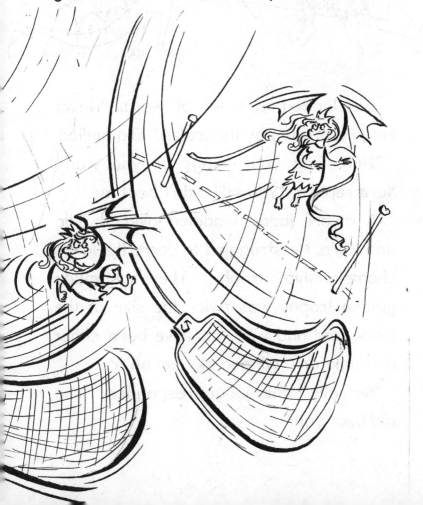

Ella landed in front of Xara. "Never judge a dragon by its scales." Ella smiled.

"Huh. Flap your wings all you want," Xara replied. "You still didn't beat me."

A dwarf judge waddled over to Ella and Xara. He struggled to carry the large championship trophy. The handmade golden trophy was twice the size of the judge and had what could've been either an eagle or a winged sky eel on top.

"Actually," the judge responded, "she *did* beat you."

"WHAT?!" a voice shouted from the crowd. Grimly the gnome pushed his way through the spectators. "Xara is the best! No one can beat her!"

The judge pulled out a very tiny hourglass and held it up. "While both contestants successfully dodged all the obstacles," the judge declared, "Ella was faster. She beat Xara by 152 grains of sand! Ella is officially the new Winged Wonders Flying Champion!"

The judge leaned over to Ella and whispered, "Erm, you *are* Ella, right? It's hard to tell with the princess dress and crown and stuff."

"You bet I am!" Ella said cheerfully. "It's going to take more than squishy skin and a very strange haircut to hold me back!"

"You did it, Ella!" Owen cheered. "You're the new Winged Wonders Flying Championship Champion!"

Owen hugged his sister. His nose wrinkled. "I didn't realize humans were so . . . squishy," he said.

"Great fireballs, that was some awesome flying!" Avalon said to Ella. "You totally deserved to win."

"And sorry for laughing at you," Fangnir said. "You're right. We shouldn't judge someone by the color of their scales, or um, if they even have any, I guess."

"Well, now that we've all hugged and learned our special lessons, don't start thinking you're gonna ever beat me again!" Xara angrily blew fire. She flapped her mighty wings and disappeared into the mountain mists.

"Well, someone's a champion sore loser," Owen said with a chuckle.

"Now can we please go see Ken?" Ella said. "If you think wearing a human princess dress is bad . . . trying wearing their underwear!"

"**D**RAGON KA-ZOWIE! ADD SOME EXTRA POWIE!"

Ken waved a new wand in circles. "Do you like it?" he asked Owen. "I just got it on sale at Wands 'R' Us."

A bolt of magic energy shot out and covered Ella. When the light faded, Ella was her normal, dragon self.

"I've got a tail?!" Ella gasped.

"Check!" Owen said.

"And scales and wings!" Ella cheered.

"Hey, my foot is back to normal, too!" Ken said. "Man, do I like this new wand!"

"It's so GOOD to be me again!" Ella sighed. "Although I'm gonna kinda miss that crown."

"Yay. Great. You're all dragony again. And just as annoying as ever. Now, please go away," Ken grumbled.

"With pleasure!" Ella said.

But as she and Owen were about to leave, Squeaky popped out from behind a black cauldron. He raced over to Owen and gave him a hug.

"Maaana meeta moo moo!" Squeaky blubbered and started to cry. *HOOOONK!* He blew his nose on Owen's wing.

"YOU!" Ella shouted. "This whole thing was all YOUR fault!"

"It wasn't, Sis! I promise!" Owen said. "Squeaky let me trade him to Ken so he'd turn you back into a dragon!"

"R-really?" Ella was shocked Squeaky would do such a nice thing. "I don't know what to say. . . ."

"How about 'Bye, Ken! Me and my annoying brother will be leaving now!'" Ken tried to push Ella and Owen right out of his stall.

"Wait!" Ella said.

"Sorry! Can't hear you! Too busy pushing you out of my life forever and ever!" Ken grunted.

"I want to trade you something to get back Squeaky," Ella said, surprising Owen and Squeaky.

"Let's see, what can you give me for the gremlin?" Ken asked. "Oh, I know. Leave me alone and never come back no matter what you've been turned into!"

"So, all we have to do is leave you alone and you'll give us back Squeaky?" Owen couldn't believe it!

"Yes!" Ken assured him. "That and give me the big golden trophy."

"That's the Winged Wonders Flying Championship Trophy!" Owen gasped. "There is no way we'll trade you that!"

"DEAL!" Ella said.

Ken shoved Squeaky into Ella's hands, grabbed the trophy, and slammed down a CLOSED sign on the table.

"Goodbye!" Ken said and disappeared in a big puff of smoke that smelled like rotten eggs.

Squeaky hugged Ella. "Meeee maaata mee booooo!"

"Sis . . . I can't believe you traded your trophy. . . ." Owen was stunned.

"If Squeaky didn't turn me into a princess," Ella began, "and I don't think he did—if he let himself be traded to a grumpy wizard like Ken—"

"I'm NOT grumpy!" Ken shouted from somewhere in the distance.

"Then whomever *did* put that curse on me is still out there and I'm gonna need all the help I can get to find him or her . . . or it . . . or that . . . or whatever they are," Ella explained.

"Then what are we waiting for?!"
Squeaky hopped up on Owen's back.
"Let's go show him or her . . . or it . . . or
that . . . or whatever . . . no one messes
with a dragon!"

"Especially *twin* dragons!" Ella cheered as they flew into the sky, never realizing that something close by in the bushes was watching their every move. And that something had been watching them ever since the Dragon Games had started. . . .

Read on for a sneak peek from an
upcoming series, *Isle of Misfits*

Isle of
MISFITS
FIRST CLASS

by JAMIE MAE   illustrated by FREYA HARTAS

BOOK
1

— chapter one —

THE LONELIEST GARGOYLE

Gibbon the gargoyle lived atop the same castle all his life. Gargoyles were meant to protect the buildings they lived on. Sometimes, that meant protecting the people inside those buildings, too. That's what Gibbon was always taught.

But Gibbon couldn't stay still in one place *all* day. Sure, it was what he was *supposed* to do, but it was so boring! So Gibbon found something new to do to pass the time: playing pranks on people as they walked by below.

And winter was his favorite season for pranks. Winter meant snowballs.

One snowy day, he saw a man in a suit hurrying by the castle. Gibbon quickly made a snowball in his hands. He held it over the edge and dropped it, watching as it hit the man right on the head.

The man jumped from the shock of the cold snow. A confused look crossed his face when he didn't see anyone around.

Holding back laughter, Gibbon rolled another snowball and dropped it on the man. This time, the man yelped and ran off.

"*Gibbon!*" a voice whispered harshly.

He jumped and turned toward the gargoyle speaking to him. Elroy was the leader of the castle gargoyles and almost never broke his silence.

"That's enough," Elroy ordered. "You are too old to be playing pranks on the humans. You need to start taking your post seriously."

"But it's so boring!" Gibbon protested. "We just stand around all day. Even at night, we do nothing! Who are we even defending the castle from anyway?"

Elroy did not move, but his eyes glared over at Gibbon. "You need to learn how to work with your team, Gibbon. Your slacking off only makes it harder for the rest of us."

With a sigh, Gibbon looked down at the street. He watched as a group of kids stopped below the castle. One of them picked up some snow and threw it at another. Instead of getting mad, the other kid started laughing and made his own snowball. In no time at all, the kids were in a full-fledged snowball fight!

That's what I want, Gibbon thought. For a very long time, Gibbon watched people's lives from the top of the castle. A lot of them had friends and family and fun, but Gibbon didn't really have any of that on the castle. The other gargoyles never wanted to play or laugh. They only wanted to watch the world as it went by.

Maybe if I can get Elroy to play, everyone else will loosen up! he thought.

Gibbon smiled at Elroy. "Hey, catch me if you can! If you do, I'll be quiet and guard the castle the rest of the day!"

With a laugh, Gibbon took off. He climbed down the side of the castle, then darted down an empty street.

Gibbon knew—he just *knew*—if Elroy played with him, he'd understand.

But when he stopped and looked back, he didn't see Elroy. His heart sank.

Journey to some magical places and outer space, rock out, and find your inner superhero with these other chapter book series from **Little Bee Books**!

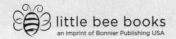

little bee books
an imprint of Bonnier Publishing USA